People at Work

Working at a School

by Connor Stratton

FOCUS READERS

SCOUT

www.focusreaders.com

Focus Readers is distributed by North Star Editions:
sales@northstareditions.com | 888-417-0195

Produced for Focus Readers by Red Line Editorial.

Photographs ©: monkeybusinessimages/iStockphoto, cover, 1; wavebreakmedia/Shutterstock Images, 4; Monkey Business Images/Shutterstock Images, 7 (top), 13, 16 (top left), 16 (bottom right); sirtravelalot/Shutterstock Images, 7 (bottom); Tyler Olson/Shutterstock Images, 9; Photgraphee.eu/Shutterstock Images, 11; Fat Camera/iStockphoto, 15; donatas1205/Shutterstock Images, 16 (bottom left); Professor25/iStockphoto, 16 (top right)

Library of Congress Cataloging-in-Publication Data
Library of Congress Cataloging-in-Publication Data is available on the Library of Congress website.

ISBN
978-1-64493-016-8 (hardcover)
978-1-64493-095-3 (paperback)
978-1-64493-253-7 (ebook pdf)
978-1-64493-174-5 (hosted ebook)

Printed in the United States of America
Mankato, MN
012020

About the Author

Connor Stratton enjoys learning new things, eating popcorn, and watching movies with friends. He lives in Minnesota.

Table of Contents

teacher

Teachers at School

Many people work
at school.
Teachers work at school.
They teach us to write.

Our teacher helps us learn.

We learn about **art**.

We learn about music.

art

Always Learning

Librarians work at school.

They teach us about **books**.

They teach us

about reading.

librarian
book

Counselors work at school.
They teach us
about **feelings**.
They teach us
about ourselves.

counselor

School Helpers

Cooks work at school.

They make us **lunch**.

cook
lunch

Nurses work at school.

They help when we are sick.

They help when we are hurt.

They help us feel better.

nurse

Glossary

art

feelings

books

lunch

Index